Red Things

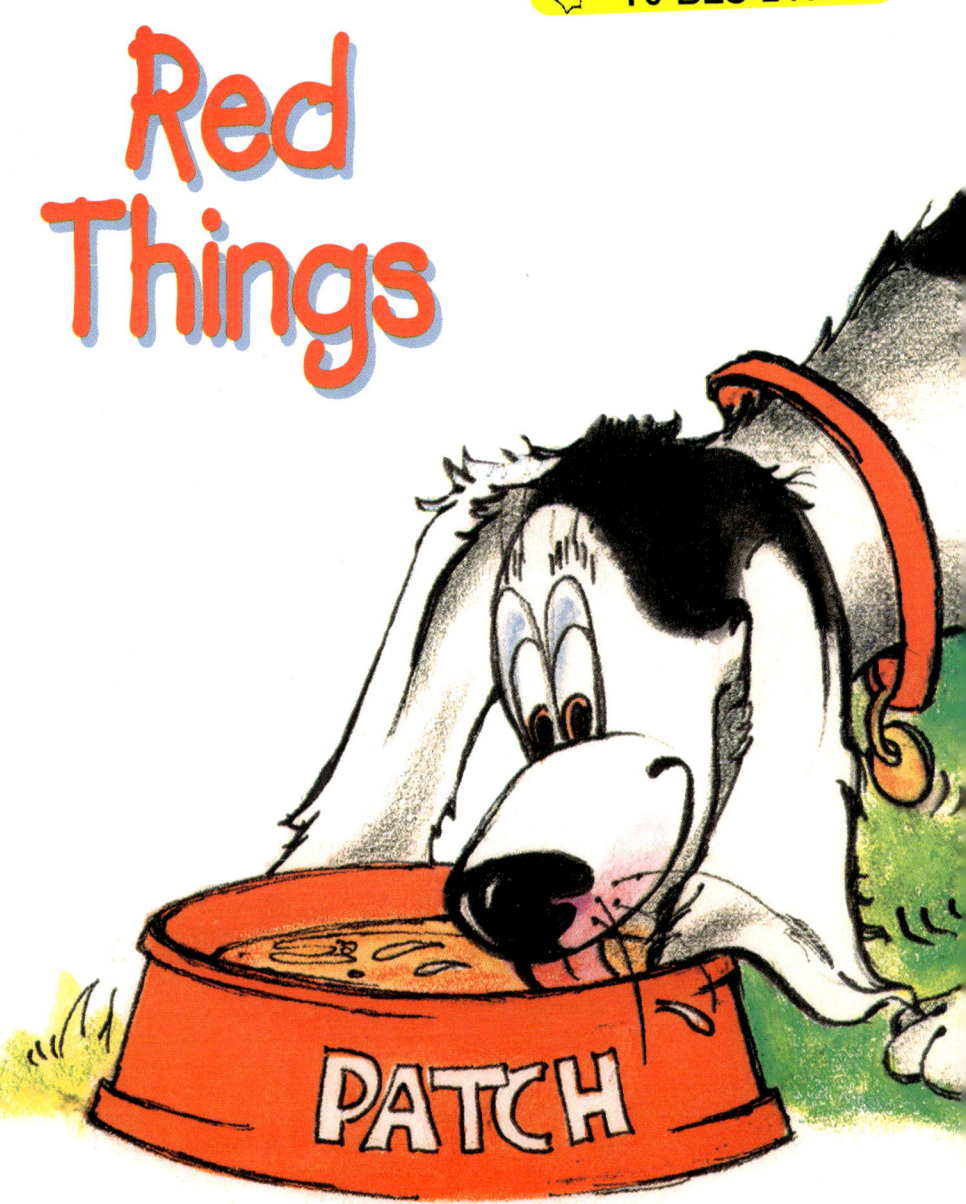

Gordon Winch & Gregory Blaxell
Illustrated by Hanna Bilyk

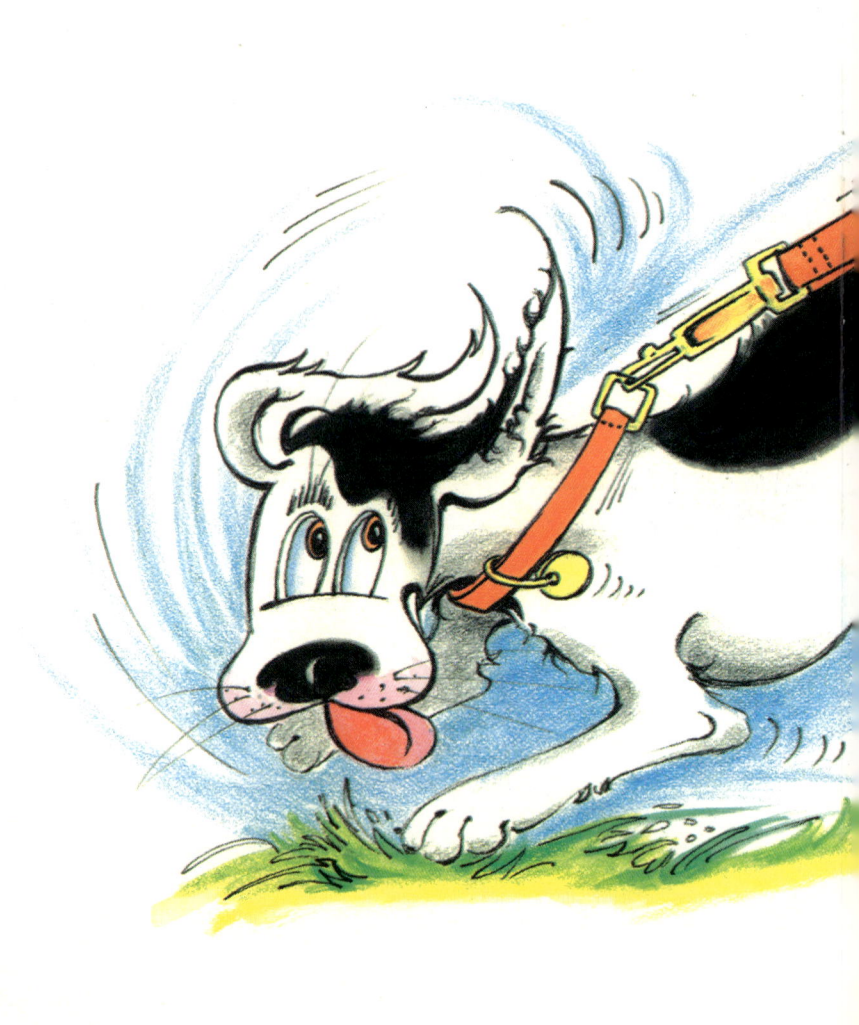

Patch has a red collar

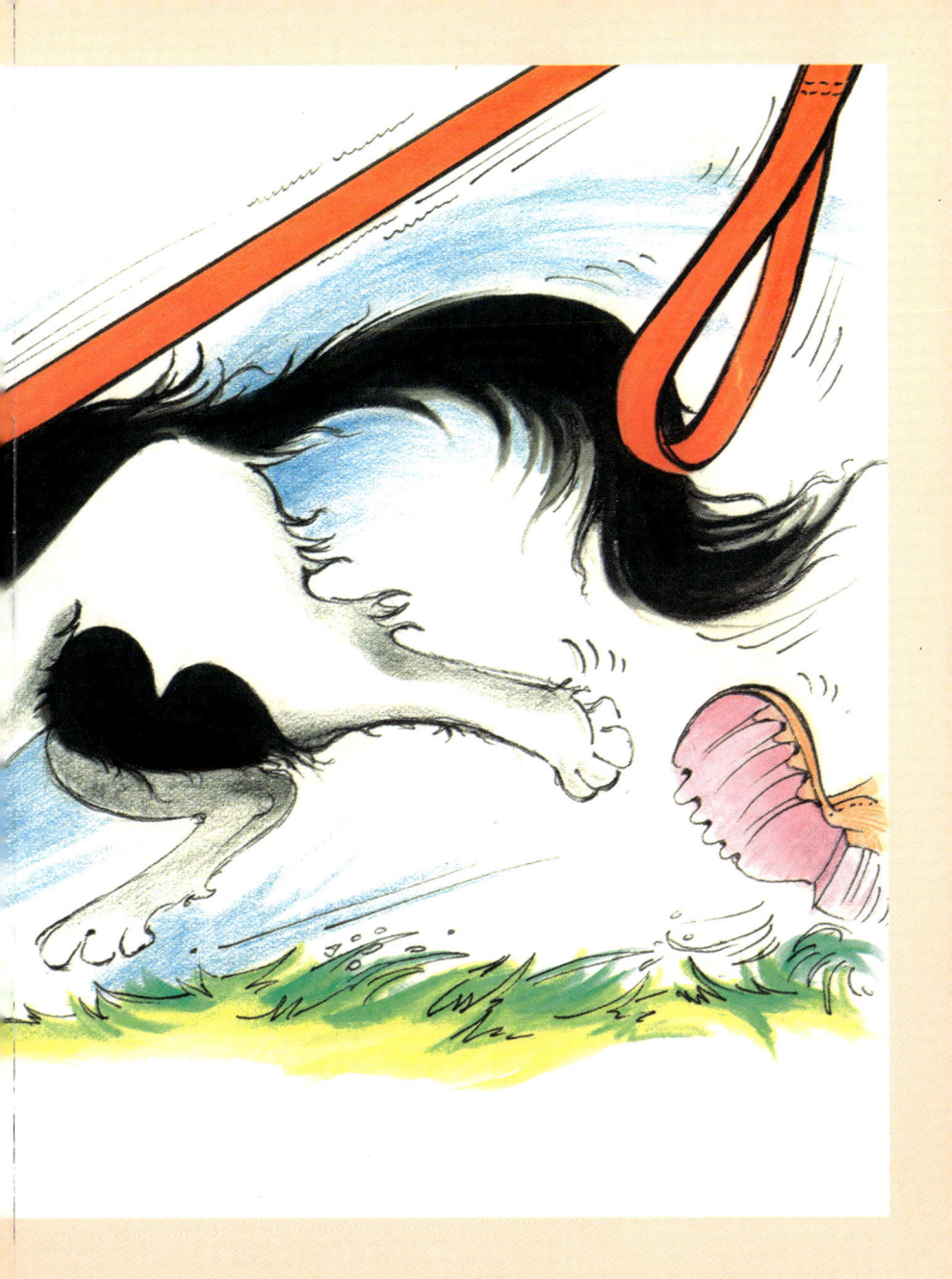

and a red leash.

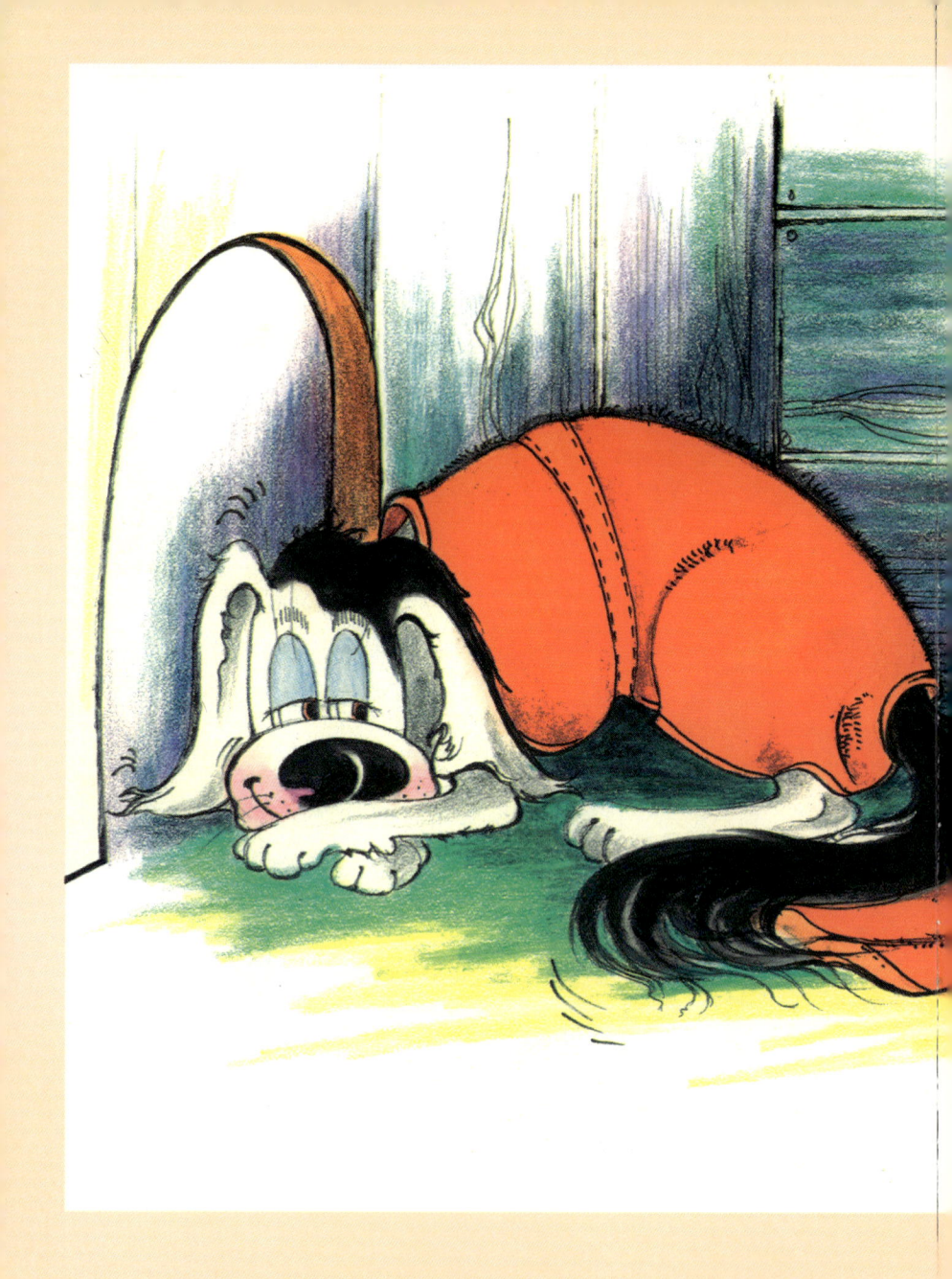

Patch has a red coat

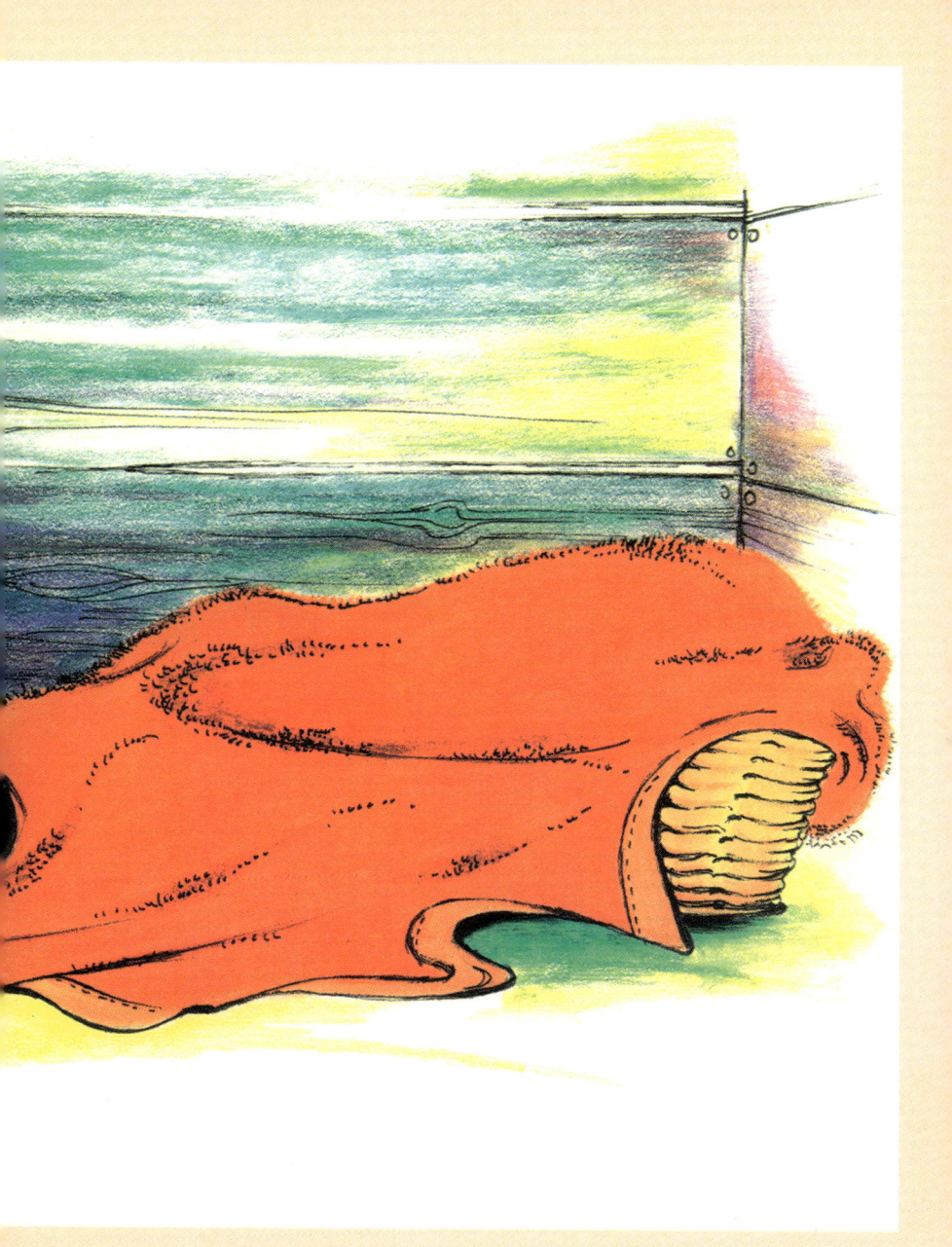

and a red bed.

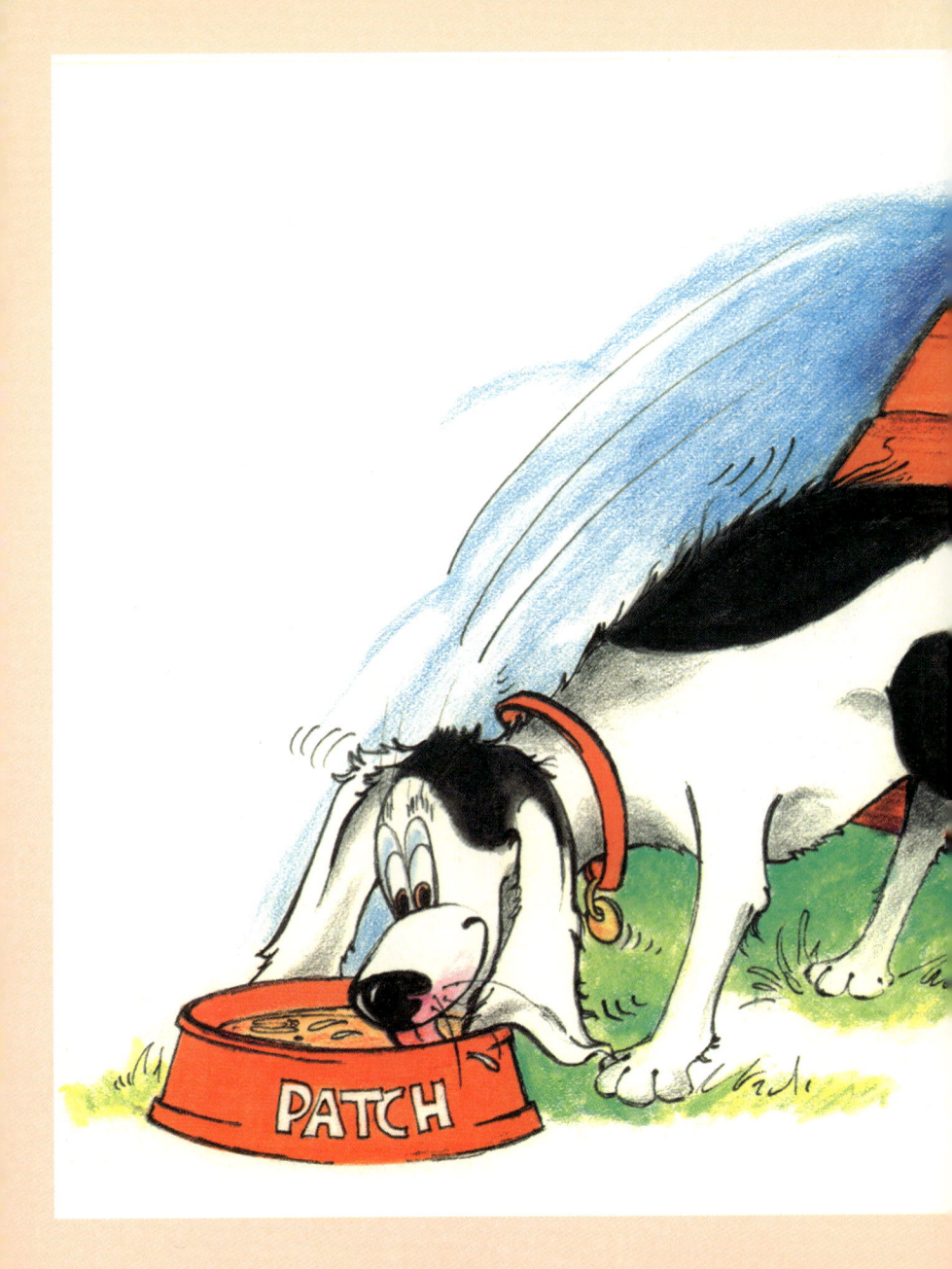

Patch has a red dish

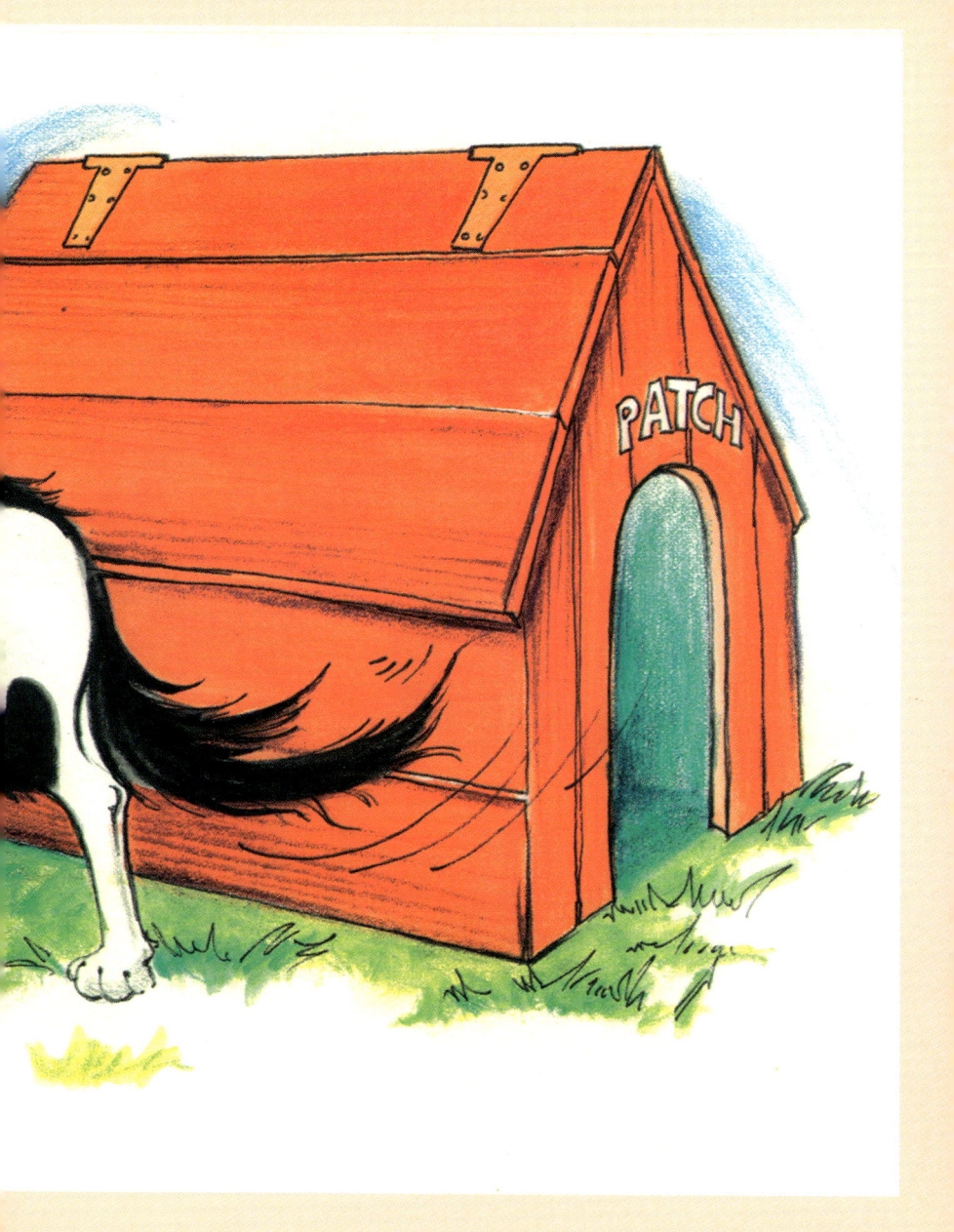

and a red doghouse.

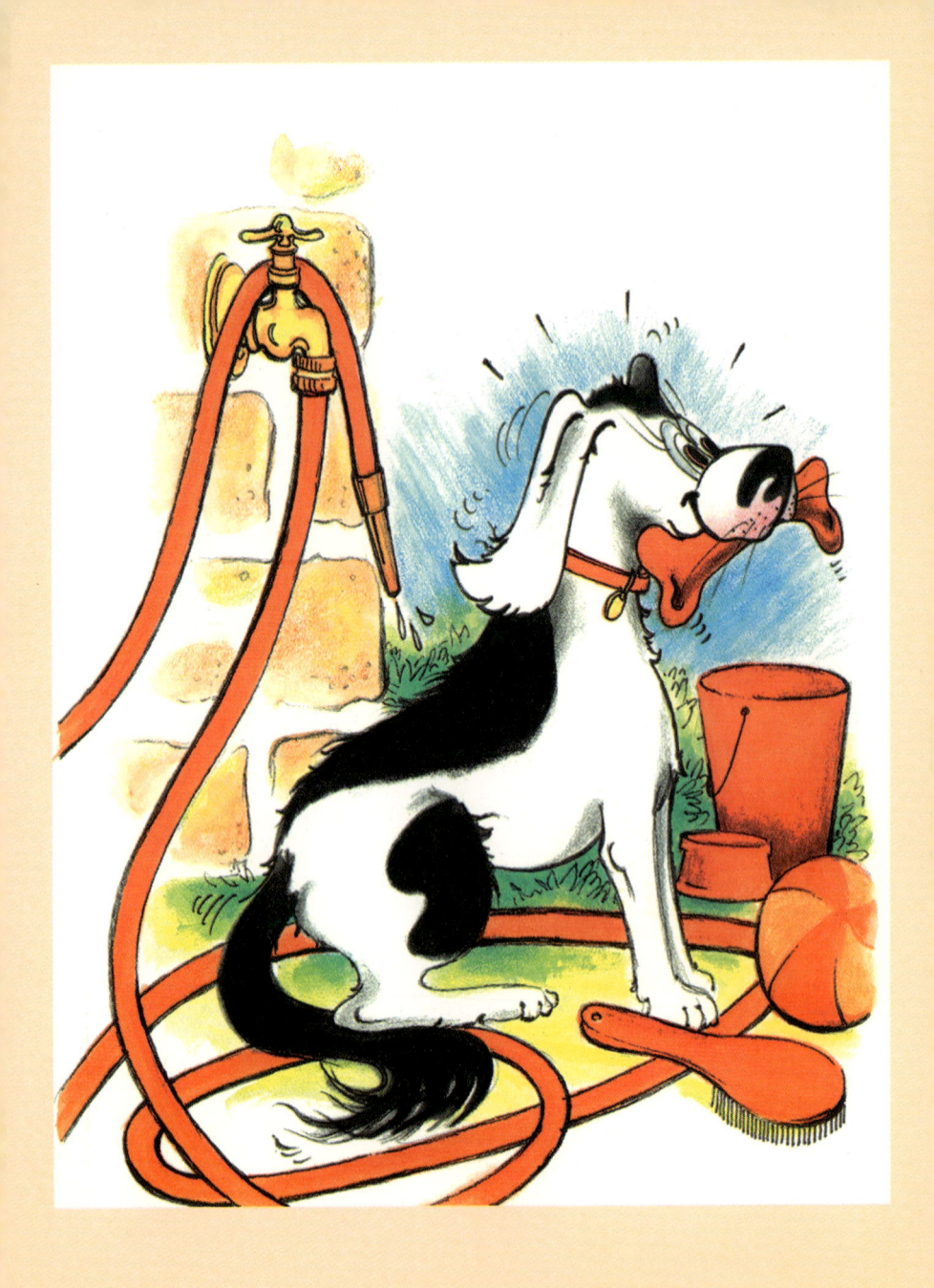

Patch likes red things.